The Fancy Witch

by Liza Charlesworth
illustrated by Zihua Yang

ISBN: 979-8-225-02078-1

Publisher: Tara Welty
Creative Director: Tannaz Fassihi; Designer: Cynthia Ng

1 2 3 4 5 6 7 8 9 10 68 34 33 32 31 30 29 28 27 26 25

Made in Jiaxing City, China. First printing, August 2025.

SCHOLASTIC

Meet a fancy witch named Wendy.
Wendy had a fine dress made of silk.
Wendy had a tall hat with a purple rose.
Wendy also had a brand-new broom,
made out of gold, that was able to zoom
more than 100 miles per hour. Wowie!

Meet a witch by the name of Gertrude.
Gertrude had a plain dress with a brown belt.
Gertrude had a crooked hat with patches.
And she did not even own a broom.
What did she ride on? An old mop that
was as slow as a flying snail.

The two witches had side-by-side homes on Cobweb Lane and were best pals. They wore their cloaks to take long walks. They wore their sneakers to jog in the park. There was just one teeny-weeny problem: Wendy felt that her things were better than Gertrude's things. Yup, Wendy was a snob.

One day, the two pals got a nice surprise.
Both of them were invited to Witch Fest
at the spooky mansion in the dark forest.
Witch Fest was a big, fantastic party with
spells and snacks and tunes and dancing.
"Yay, I cannot wait!" exclaimed Gertrude.
"Yes, indeed!" said Wendy. "And who will
be the fanciest witch at the party? ME!"

What did Wendy do to get set for Witch Fest?
She curled her hair and pressed her silk dress.
She put on a necklace with big, sparkly gems.
She polished her golden broom until it gleamed.
What did Gertrude do to get set for the party?
Not one thing. “I like myself the way I am,”
she declared with a smile.

On the big night of Witch Fest, Wendy and Gertrude met up on the sidewalk. The party was 100 miles away so Wendy had her broom and Gertrude had her mop.
"You look terrific!" exclaimed Gertrude.
"And you look like. . .you," replied Wendy, wrinkling up her perfect blue nose.

Then Wendy added, “Please do NOT tell me you are planning to ride on that old mop.”
“Yes, I am,” stated Gertrude with a grin.
“This old mop has never let me down.
“Well, if that is the case,” said Wendy,
“we cannot fly together. I will NOT be seen with you on that horrible thing!”
Plus, my golden broom is as fast as the wind.
So, I’ll just have to meet you at the party.”

After that, Wendy waved her fancy blue hand and flew quickly away. Zip, zap, zoom! "OK. Bye! See you soon!" yelled Gertrude. Did she feel hurt? Yes. Did Wendy's mean words keep Gertrude from Witch Fest? No way! She hopped on her old mop and lifted off into the dark sky.

Gertrude's vehicle was not fast or fancy, but she enjoyed the ride. Up, up she flew—higher than the pine trees and black bats. Far away in the distance, she was able to spot Wendy on her fine golden broom—zooming into the bright light of the moon.

Gertrude flew and flew and flew and flew. She was just a few miles from Witch Fest when she spotted a VERY scary sight. It wasn't a ghost or goblin. It was Wendy! She was hanging onto the thin branch of a tree and screaming at the top of her lungs: "GERTRUDE, PLEASE, PLEASE, HELP ME!"

Did Gertrude think twice? Nope, she did not. Her best pal was in danger and she needed to help her—quickly! So she backed her mop right up to the tree and yelled, “Hop on, pal. My mop isn’t golden, but it’s got lots of room.” Did Wendy think twice? Nope, she did not.

She hopped on the old mop. Zip, zap, zoom! She did so just before the branch snapped and fell to the ground with a loud CRASH! When the two witches looked down—YIKES! They saw that the branch had landed right next to Wendy's quite-broken golden broom.

"What a trip!" exclaimed Wendy when they finally got to Witch Fest. "My golden broom may have looked fancy, but it was a dud. In the middle of the woods, it took a nose-dive. Thank goodness, I grabbed the tree branch! Thank goodness, too, my best pal flew by! You and your old mop saved my life. I am sorry I was so rude and snobby."

"Thanks for the apology," Gertrude replied. "My mop may be old and slow as a snail, but it has never, ever, ever let me down." As the two pals walked toward the party, Wendy said, "My fancy dress is torn and my hair is a huge mess. But do I mind? Not a bit! It feels good to arrive. . . with my bestie by my side."

Then Wendy and Gertrude opened the creaky door of the spooky mansion and went inside. Wowie! There were yummy snacks and games and a cool goblin DJ playing hip-hop tunes. So, they hit the dance floor. Zip, zap, zoom!